W9-CES-946

DRAGONS

DRAGON LIFE

by Matt Doeden
illustrated by Jonathan Mayer

Consultant
Dr. Peter Hogarth
Professor, Department of Biology
University of York, United Kingdom

Mankato, Minnesota

Edge Books are published by Capstone Press,
151 Good Counsel Drive, P.O. Box 669, Mankato, Minnesota 56002.
www.capstonepress.com

Printed in the United States of America

Library of Congress Cataloging-in-Publication Data
Doeden, Matt.
Dragon life / by Matt Doeden; illustrated by Jonathan Mayer.
p. cm. – (Edge books. Dragons)
Summary: "Describes natural dragon behaviors and habitats. Includes a photo-glossary describing the appearance and characteristics of several dragon species" – Provided by publisher.
Includes bibliographical references and index.
ISBN–13: 978-1-4296-1297-5 (hardcover)
ISBN–10: 1-4296-1297-5 (hardcover)
1. Dragons – Juvenile literature. I. Mayer, Jonathan, 1984– ill. II. Title. III. Series.
GR830.D7D634 2008
398.24'54 – dc22 2007025097

Editorial Credits
Aaron Sautter, editor; Ted Williams, designer

Photo Credits
Shutterstock/abzora, backgrounds; Andrey Zyk, backgrounds

1 2 3 4 5 6 13 12 11 10 09 08

Table of Contents

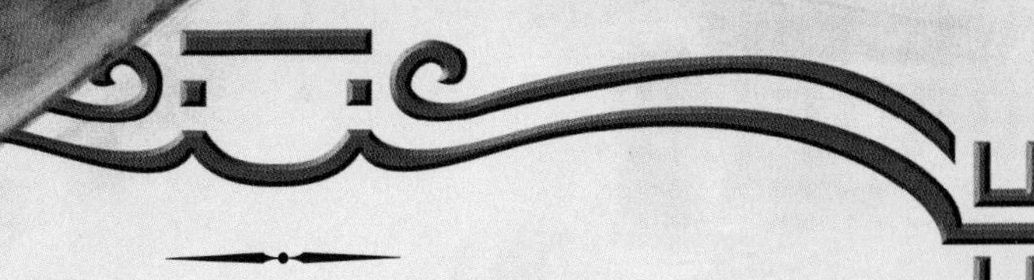

CHAPTER ONE

AN EASY MEAL

A young dragon wakes up with a fierce hunger. Slowly, it stands and stretches. Its great wings can barely open inside its cave. As its wings spread, coins, gems, and other treasures spill off of them. The dragon's **hoard** is growing, as is the dragon itself. Soon, it will be time for the dragon to find a new **lair**.

The sun sets as the dragon crawls from the cave's hidden entrance. It leaps from the cliffside into the air. The dragon thinks about hunting for some deer, but it's too hungry. It needs to eat now. Instead, the dragon flies to a nearby farm, where it spies a flock of juicy sheep. The dragon dives, snapping up one of the animals in its powerful jaws. Within seconds, it swallows the sheep whole. It turns to grab another.

hoard – the treasure collected by a dragon
lair – a place where a wild animal lives and sleeps

Two farmers rush out with swords and spears to protect their sheep. The dragon laughs at the helpless humans. Their tiny weapons are no danger to the dragon's armored scales. Its fiery breath could easily burn the men where they stand. But even though they are no threat, the dragon knows that there are some people who are. It's best not to cause too much trouble. The dragon doesn't want to deal with a dragon slayer on the hunt. The dragon swoops down one last time, snatches another sheep, and rises into the evening sky.

Imagine if the world was filled with dragons. How would they live? What might they do? And how would people get along with the mighty beasts? If you use your imagination, it's not hard to picture a world where dragons could be more than just a myth.

DRAGON FACT

A dragon's true name is a tightly guarded secret. Rumors say that knowing a dragon's true name gives a person power over it.

CHAPTER TWO

SAFE AT HOME

Dragons can live just about anywhere. From towering mountaintops to the depths of the sea, there are dragons. They seem to be solitary creatures. They gather only to fight for territory or to mate. Beyond that, little is known about what dragon **society** is like.

The Lair

Dragons choose their lairs carefully. They need plenty of hunting ground nearby. Most dragons like the security of an enclosed lair. But at the same time, dragons need enough space to move their huge bodies around. Most importantly, dragons never move into a lair that's already in a more powerful dragon's territory. That can be a deadly mistake.

society – a group that shares the same laws and customs

Dragon lairs vary by type, or species, of dragon. The most common lairs are found in deep underground caves. Caves are like forts for dragons. They are safe places to sleep, which dragons do for weeks or months at a time. Even water dragons prefer underwater caves. Other dragon lairs include swamps and abandoned castles.

A dragon's lair must be large enough to contain its treasure hoard. Dragons believe that treasure gives them power. Almost all dragons collect treasure of some sort. They believe that the more treasure they have, the more powerful they become. Gold, silver, and gems are just a few examples of dragon treasure. Many water dragons collect pearls. Magical objects like enchanted swords and magic rings are highly prized by most dragons too.

Dragons and People

Normally, dragons and people are enemies. Dragons love feasting on sheep, pigs, cattle, and other farm animals. Their taste for this easy prey makes them especially unpopular with farmers. They also destroy towns and villages while looking for treasure to add to their hoards. Dragon slayers are often called to rid kingdoms of dangerous dragons. Some slayers have succeeded, but many have failed and lost their lives in the process.

DRAGON FACT

Dragons can hypnotize people and control their thoughts with a single look. People hypnotized this way are under the "dragon's spell."

Usually, people live as far from dragons as possible. But sometimes dragons and people do get along. Some dragons even learn human languages so they can share their vast knowledge and wisdom. In some cases, dragons share a close bond with a person. They'll even let that person ride on them. On rare occasions, dragons will even use their magical abilities to help people special to them.

Chapter Three

A Dragon's Life

Dragons are mysterious creatures of the imagination. People will never fully understand them. But if dragons were real, people could watch them to get a glimpse into their daily lives.

On the Hunt

Few sights are as fantastic as a dragon on the hunt. All dragons are meat-eaters, or **carnivores**. Most dragons are happy snacking on farm animals. But dragon slayers can make it hard for dragons to grab this easy prey. Dragons often have to hunt for other food. They will eat deer, buffalo, and other large animals. Some even hunt elephants.

Most dragons hunt alone. Like eagles or hawks, many dragons fly high to search for prey. When they find food, they dive out of the sky to capture it. Before eating, some dragons like to roast their prey with their fiery breath. But in most cases, dragons simply swallow their food whole.

carnivore – an animal that eats meat

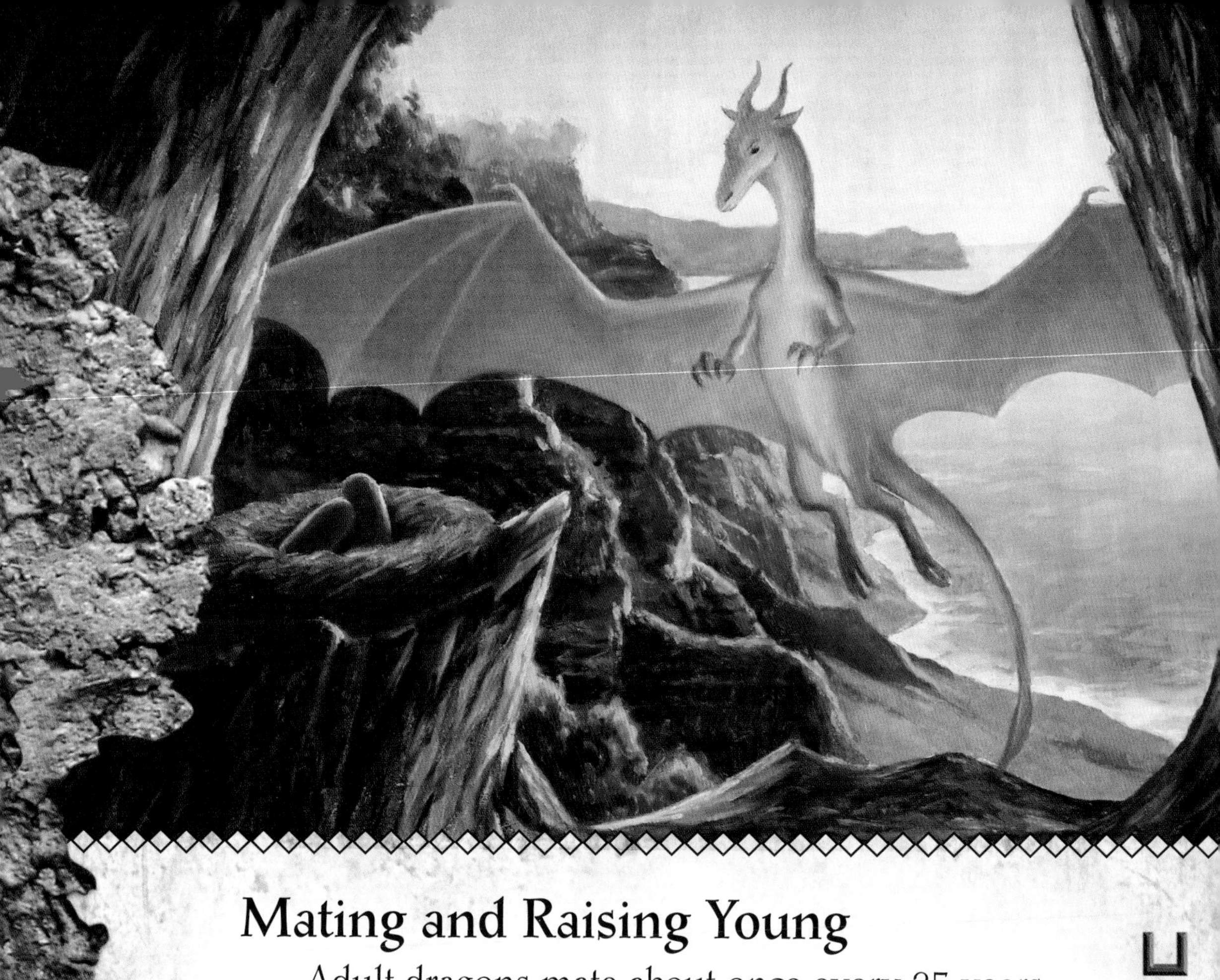

Mating and Raising Young

Adult dragons mate about once every 25 years. Flying dragons have an amazing mating dance. The dragons grasp each other's talons, wrap their wings around each other, and dive steeply toward the ground. Just before they hit the ground, they swoop back into the sky and fly off to find a nesting place.

Like most reptiles, dragons lay eggs. Females lay **clutches** of eggs in their lairs. Clutches may contain up to three eggs. Females usually guard the eggs and stay with the hatchlings until they can fly. But males may sometimes help guard the young.

clutch – a group of eggs in a nest

At first, dragon hatchlings are helpless. Their scales are soft, and their wings aren't fully developed. But they grow quickly. In about a year, the young dragons live on their own. They learn to hunt and take care of themselves. They search for a lair of their own so they can start collecting treasure.

The first few years are dangerous for young dragons. Powerful adult dragons and dragon slayers often kill young dragons before they can reach adulthood. Only about one out of 10 dragons live to become adults. But the strong survivors can look forward to long lives as the king of mythical beasts.

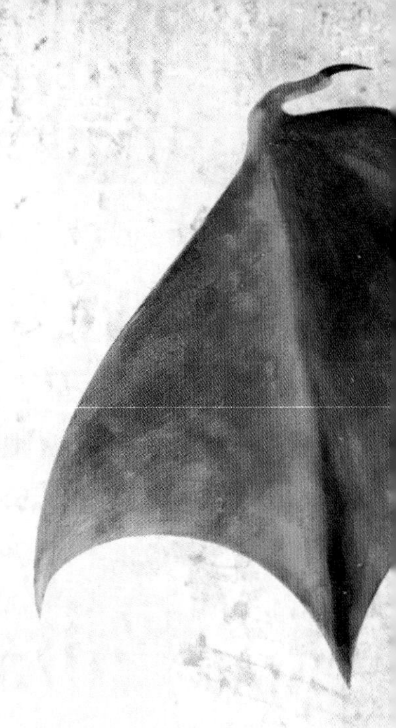

CHAPTER FOUR

TYPES OF DRAGONS

Though dragons are imaginary beasts, they come in many shapes and sizes. Each dragon species has its own unique features. Some dragons breathe fire, while others have an icy blast. Some can fly, while others swim in lakes or oceans. This illustrated guide can help you identify almost any type of dragon.

Wyvern

Wyverns live in the wildest parts of Africa. They are the largest of all dragons. They have two large wings and two feet tipped with eaglelike talons.

Size: *Up to 50 feet (15 meters) long and 25 feet (8 meters) tall*
Home: *Rocky cliffs, sand dunes, and grassy plains*
Colors: *Usually brown or green*
Natural Weapons: *Poisonous breath and sharp talons*
Prey: *Large animals like elephants or hippopotamuses*

Western Dragon

Western dragons are found mostly in the mountains of Europe. They have two large batlike wings, four clawed feet, and a long arrowhead-shaped tail.

Size: *Up to 45 feet (14 meters) long and 17 feet (5 meters) tall*
Home: *Mountain caves or empty castles*
Colors: *Red, green, black, or gold*
Natural Weapons: *Fiery breath, claws, and a powerful tail*
Prey: *Deer, sheep, cattle, and sometimes humans*

Frost Dragon

Frost dragons are similar in size and appearance to western dragons. The biggest difference is their ability to instantly freeze their enemies with their icy breath.

Size: *Up to 45 feet (14 meters) long and 17 feet (5 meters) tall*
Home: *Icy caves in mountains or glaciers*
Colors: *Usually white or light blue*
Natural Weapons: *Icy breath, claws, and a powerful tail*
Prey: *Polar bears, seals, and sea creatures*

Amphithere

Amphitheres are known for their brightly colored feathers. They often live in temple ruins in South America. They have strong, whiplike tails.

Size: *Up to 45 feet (14 meters) long and 10 feet (3 meters) tall*
Home: *Lake islands and temple ruins*
Colors: *Bright blue with some green feathers*
Natural Weapons: *Fiery breath and a strong tail*
Prey: *Llamas, elk, bison, and other large animals*

Eastern Dragon

Eastern dragons are rarely evil and don't collect treasure. They don't have wings. But they usually carry large magic pearls, which give them the ability to fly.

Size: *Up to 40 feet (12 meters) long and 15 feet (5 meters) tall*
Home: *Underwater caves*
Colors: *Black, blue, red, white, or yellow*
Natural Weapons:
Teeth, claws, and horns
Prey: *Fish and birds*

Lindwyrm

Lindwyrms are wingless dragons that look like huge snakes. Some lindwyrms have two tiny feet that are almost useless. They usually live on grassy plains in Europe.

Size: *Up to 35 feet (11 meters) long and 10 feet (3 meters) tall*
Home: *Small caves next to streams and rivers*
Colors: *Pale green or sandy yellow*
Natural Weapons: *Poisonous bite and constriction*
Prey: *Deer, rabbits, and sometimes humans*

KNUCKER

Knuckers are related to lindwyrms, but they have four feet and two tiny, useless wings. They live mostly in ponds and swamps in Europe.

Size: *Up to 30 feet (9 meters) long and 6 feet (2 meters) tall*
Home: *Ponds, swamps, or the bottoms of wells*
Colors: *Usually red, brown, or green*
Natural Weapons: *Poisonous bite and constriction*
Prey: *Rabbits, squirrels, and sometimes humans*

DRAKE

Drakes are wingless cousins of western dragons. They are dangerous beasts that fiercely guard their treasure. They live mostly in northern Europe.

Size: *Up to 45 feet (14 meters) long and 15 feet (5 meters) tall*
Home: *Mountain caves*
Colors: *Steely gray, red, green, or brown*
Natural Weapons: *Fiery breath, claws, and a powerful tail*
Prey: *Almost any animal, sometimes humans*

Water Dragon

Water dragons are fierce sea predators. Their back feet are shaped like fins. A few have tiny wings, but they can't fly. They are found in oceans around the world.

Size: *Up to 35 feet (11 meters) long and 10 feet (3 meters) tall*
Home: *Underwater caves on the coast*
Colors: *Usually blue or gray*
Natural Weapons:
Teeth, poisonous bite, and front claws
Prey: *Mostly fish, but sometimes sailors*

COCKATRICE

The cockatrice is a strange beast that is related to dragons. It looks like a large rooster, but it also has dragonlike features. The cockatrice can turn victims to stone with a single look.

Size: *About 3 feet (1 meter) tall*
Home: *Nests in forest trees*
Colors: *Brown or red feathers with gray scales*
Natural Weapons: *Poisonous breath, turns victims to stone*
Prey: *Almost any small animal or bird*

Hydra

The hydra is a wingless, many-headed dragon. It's said that if one hydra head is cut off, two more grow back in its place. Hydras are very difficult to kill.

Size: *Up to 30 feet (9 meters) long and 12 feet (4 meters) tall*
Home: *Underwater caves behind waterfalls*
Colors: *Usually blue or green*
Natural Weapons: *Fire, ice, or poisonous breath, claws, and teeth*
Prey: *Fish, small animals, and humans*

Glossary

carnivore (KAR-nuh-vor) — an animal that eats meat

clutch (KLUHCH) — a group of eggs in a nest

constriction (kuhn-STRIK-shuhn) — the process of squeezing an animal to death

hatchling (HACH-ling) — a recently hatched dragon

hoard (HORD) — the treasure collected by a dragon

hypnotize (HIP-nuh-tize) — to put a person in a sleeplike state

lair (LAIR) — a place where a wild animal lives and sleeps

society (suh-SYE-uh-tee) — a group that shares the same laws and customs

species (SPEE-sheez) — a group of plants or animals that share common features

talon (TAL-uhn) — a long, sharp claw

Read More

Ciruelo. *The Book of the Dragon.* New York: Union Square Press, 2005.

Hamilton, John. *Dragons.* Fantasy and Folklore. Edina, Minn.: Abdo, 2005.

Steer, Dugald, ed. *Dr. Ernest Drake's Dragonology Handbook: A Practical Course in Dragons.* Cambridge, Mass.: Candlewick Press, 2005.

Internet Sites

FactHound offers a safe, fun way to find Internet sites related to this book. All of the sites on FactHound have been researched by our staff.

Here's how:

1. Visit *www.facthound.com*
2. Choose your grade level.
3. Type in this book ID code **1429612975** for age-appropriate sites. You may also browse subjects by clicking on letters, or by clicking on pictures and words.
4. Click on the **Fetch It** button.

FactHound will fetch the best sites for you!